the lives of thomas–

episodes& prayers

john high

five fingers press
san francisco
california

Many of these pieces first appeared in the Soviet journals *The Conversationalist*, *The Circus* and *Humanist* in Russian translations by Nina Iskrenko and Aleksandr Eremenko. Some of the work has also appeared in *Avec* and *Talisman*.

Five Fingers Press Book Series #3
Editors: Aleka Chase and Thoreau Lovell
Book and Cover Design: Thoreau Lovell
Cover Image and Artwork: Thomas C. Leaver

Desktop Publishing: Dave Stevenson and Grendl Moseley
Printed in Michigan by Braun-Brumfield

Five Fingers Press
P.O. Box 15426
San Francisco, CA 94115

ISBN 0-961840-96-X
Library of Congress Catalog Number 91-72643

contents

I: *tracks*

image

finney tracing maps of the nile&
red sea from old national geographics.
(1951.) that kind of ease. the drawer full
of them within an hour. how imagination
tricksters. his daddy the preacher believing
the pharisees stole the sacred scrolls from the
river. carting them off to the dead sea when
his mississippi was so much more alive. hep
man. hep man thomas they called him. daddy to them
all. crocodile king. the faint lines blackening around
the edge of a folded page. finney's worlds taking
shape. catfish in the waters. all the fragments.
then a half-cracked bowl. the gold
fish flickering across the maps as the waters
pour forth& go lost. a treasure in his field without
knowing it. finney almost empty as the pencil is
laid on the table. accomplished in these beginnings.

a movement& a rest

the bad ju ju is what the eye wants
our old lives no longer
requiring attention. they possess
so many fields
—have you discovered the beginning so that
you inquire about the end?
not that their love
the cha cha midnight of quiet
evenings is over (us)
—you make eyes in the place of an eye then?
charlie hypnotized by a slight hum
change the dial on the radio he says
no more of that nashville shit
finney doubled in language by this repose
that loves us for no reason
at all
darkness inside of darkness
the many who are first will become last
you made it alive
pissing up& down this road

hitchhikers

P.S. Charlie, don't lie.

I. the highway

November already. Charlie, I mostly picture her when I think of last Christmas, on the road together—that map of the world she handed over while standing on the corner of Burn& Maple, scratching her thighs like a miniature cat and that was somewhere south of Toledo. The partially gutted-out hotel off Route 90, *The Bosie Hex* it was called, where we opened pawn store gifts. The thick shades she bought me in the dead of winter and the pair of blue alligator high heels I swore we stole her while gigging my way through Florida& (I never been to Florida and she knew that, Charlie). We bundled tight against the cold, fucking early, smoking brown cigars no bigger than baby fingers, drinking cheap holiday champagne and pretending to listen to the imaginary silence, the scarred hobo hooting& cat calls& the neon flicker of the drugstore mall. Fingering my sax she had me scoot it between her legs hawking a Parker tune all dizzy and later she called home to her sister but she don't have a sister Charlie and you know that& we didn't have the vaguest as to how to approach it. Those mornings she woke kissing me all over, that perfect o-ring sexy mouth, as if it were she who breathed out the almost warm January winds that came with us across the great plains. I can honestly say she was thankful, Charlie. Even appreciative I'd returned from Ohio& left you for whatever— choose your luck, so drunk I'd never believe anything you said, spitting out *duck their kicks& still crawl up their legs* as if it

meant something? Appreciative I'd come back, yes, stealing
her away from those moonshine suckers, your daddy& what
he'd do& hell no I felt no remorse not for you or him or
anyone, why should I? It was just a boot-leg on the ridge, the
old man& we can't figure you out either Charlie, so fuck it.

II. catwalking

Shit, her dancing by the side of the road.
By the time we got to Montana
winter ferns& cactus blooming out of season,
then that sudden Denver snow
crossing the Rockies.
All those white storms followed us
through the mountains
'til we made Seattle& the north woods.

her fine contours/
apparitions really
against the stage shadows/crawling
shooting beer joints& strip
halls for a few bucks
a shit palace to sleep
in

Tooting God   this is change
if you look hard enough.
Nothing like your meanness&
fear of everything out there, Charlie.
No. Go on& die. We shined it—

6

goosing love& forking all possible roads
born that way since no backsliding's
allowed& (I reminded her every damn day
no turning back)
we killed your daddy.

dear charlie,

no we didn't like those other men lumberjacks mostly eyeing
her down whistling dixie big tease snapping peep hole show
beats& my jazz like it was real our own but you know katie
always did have her own mind not to be obliging or about to
owe me& ah yes you were right charlie& no i couldn't talk her
out of nothing& yes it was her money& her body& yes you
were always right about one thing charlie i'm a fool wanted to
make it on my own& yes for both of us& yes maybe even to
come back for your drunk ass once the cash started rolling&
we set things right got a home& a place because you're still our
brother no matter& jesus did i believe jesus learning it all over
now starting from go you hear me charlie you hear me mo'
charlie you hear me

III. landscapeshoes
        (ghosted)

Down the coast
we hopped freight, laughed& joked for three weeks
dreaming up fantasies about California.

Jumped the tracks in Novato
and damn near walked twenty miles.
We figured to shake famous
if not rich by summer.
Then we knew I'd have her love.
San Francisco, the foggy beach wine nights
talk bang sugar touching strange bodies
running whores& back table dice&
my horn like a little juju
man in gold before me
leading on/shuffling/rolling
rifts with the waves& top that man
(just you top it).
Coon shit   asssassins/hundred
dollar hits/shimmied skirts&
the blind boys were all there
every night   making me think of her
black panties on the sand.
We'd kneel in the ocean
(hell, me scared of sharks)
you should have knelt down dammit!
Water washing around our waists/our sex&
practically froze my ass   lots of times—
&sure Katie had her other boys
shotgun lovers she says
so I did the same.
Seemed so easy& dying&
mirage in the window watching
her with someone (was it you Charlie)
until she decided for herself—
I was either too much of men
or not one at all.
Until she finally took jealous
like we had for almost six crazy years

seeing her other brothers, her daddy, even
you on the mattress around back
where I buried him, Charlie—
buried him that son of a bitch.
Maybe we pushed things too far
but I just watched her walk away
sun sparkling on those blue
alligator shoes.

IV. *multiple lives*

We read stories about all those fuckers jumping off the bridge.
They don't even sing. Bird boys. Flying. Claw voiced. Not me.
But three months gone now like the whole year will pass
regardless of whether she comes back. Each afternoon living
on its own. I sit here, a sliced pear lying on the magnolia desk,
that painted over mahogany dresser the two of us
discovered in Chinatown. Mornings we worked it smooth
Charlie, better than any music even—searched the pattern,
stripped it down. Staring out on those gray dusty hills/not like
home boy. Smell that lingering orange fragrance/just salt air,
sun& rain, but beautiful. Why can't we accept that?

I know one thing. It's memory that waits us, sure as the Blue
Heel I bought her, and that rotting piece of saxophone brass
leaning against the chair. Funny how I don't even want to pick
it up anymore. Watching a glare off the waves skim its way
across the blurred horizon. Blurred or blind myself, we can't
tell. Alone mostly, that's the main thing. Who can instruct us
better?

This is the story inside the story. Regardless of how I tell it. It doesn't belong to us. Anymore than you do. After all that fishing. Telling the truth?

V. the end or
(your sister lied too, Charlie)

Take imagination for example.

So what if nothing survives we say. Like you couldn't feel a knife if someone were to stab you. Pain that was not yet the pain of love. Katie shivers, looks at the fire, licks my shoulders. Our last night on the beach, me seduced by that other man? (Was it you, Charlie?) I played A Train, later Monk, sure of that. How baby hovered over my throat, talking about you, waving that knife in my face, naked herself—telling us you were already dead& later on masturbating as she calmly talked from the water. See Charlie, this is what I think. The man I was that night didn't trust death, sensed it coming but couldn't face it anymore than we could admit to never really killing her daddy or fuckin' anybody, chicken shit-faced but leaving you up there to die alone& so I got spooked, bet your ass, couldn't even play my own tunes& acting as if a lover, any lover could uncover in the sand something violent enough to interlock time—make things connect you know like notes all blending together, like our music, the way everything fell from her mouth in that moment.

Love we mean.

Love was six years of her hand always slipping between past&
present or two bodies pitched into a kind of endless solitude
together only those were her bodies& you were in one of
them& we were just the past approaching dream Charlie,
that's all.

The three of us lingered awhile
studied this handsome figure
just swimming the waves, sandpipers&
fish eyes turning on the surf's edge&
then the pigeons& that mysterious swimmer&
bopping in the water as she scopes me, saying
hush, it's ok—you got dreams as big
as the darkness, don't you?
Sure I answer.
Sure we do.
Did she really talk that way, Charlie?
(Did we?)
A complete black, moontide
water shy then crashing.
A faint cry   lifting   from   a small mouth.
Did we know what she was saying?
Could I understand her, or us, or any of this shit
even now?

Have you seen her, Charlie? Come on, tell us this time, who
chose this face?

off route 90

the weeks begin slowly for them now. as if
in anticipation. or without any. she's forgotten
how to live. finding each turn for the image as
a blind intersection. a crossing for the past that
can't be fixed into being. thus finney's other
fiction. what they do after hours designated
by habit. the blue air separating us. intention
left alone for a moment. a night presenting
itself as the matter of factness in a lamp.
a half empty beer. a bed waiting on its own
only. &just that.

she can't dream what will become clear. the
plot suspended when what they say is simply
survive. continue. a fine voice at times. sometimes
we know love between the acts of recognition. or
the personal as you say it. where they go after
work. sodom. gomorrah. new york. memphis.
all dead names. signals. yet possibility is
it all happening tonight as she prepares the clean
pillows. waiting.

high school reunion

the domed temple we left from

—the body pretends to be the soul but it isn't finney

shadowed green& footsteps across the
dry fields

blind girls this time
walking the canals

touching mouths
then the manor brick lanes

—shoveled mounds?
yes

taking us back
ash covered
worms, talk grass
blue speckled snakes
—do you know what you're talking about?
love yes

or at your wedding feast
later that week

in the two-day air
—a blueness complete?
yes

a book of testaments
you blindfolded
following the one
once ancient
oars
rice wine, horns, cockroaches
&the small ants
all over the corpse

a quick wind
birch trees
laughing

—whose bitter mystery?

apple loaves
scattered about the oak table

what the world wants when it finds itself

playing tongues on new year's eve

tower of nimrods' origin in this tongue, our noah, flesh
of fish, moses on the bridge signaling us toward the waters,
do you remember, charlie—how they found you& finney
in a fishtrap on new year's morning—remember
our bodies covered in octopus, weeds, bass, some perch, then
the small shark you mistook as a mother as your real daddy
thomas in the shape of jesus the fisher waved us on? in the day
when you devoured the dead, you made it alive, when you come
into the light what will you do? do you hear us still? on this day
of our mutual birth& dying? on the day when you were one you
became two but when you have become two what will you do?
where to uncover the parched leaves, skins beyond the word
known to all tongues? tell us now in order to leave this, the other
fiction where we became them, can you hear us now? this the last
call, our only eyes, a final horn

II: *parables of the blind*

image

maybe they come out of this longing for an earlier
language, one still flying toward absence when in
the story the eye takes its own& leaves us. or the mixed
whatever dice tumbling, a go at the cards& then there's so
little patience for politics in the world and why not? you're
tearing the limbs away from an animal small, too delicate,
refined. a part of the loving& it doesn't grieve itself
freely. common roads on the map that lead to more
roads? ok. i admit the idiocy, take every side of it like an
unexpected plane, a slow walk, the dissuasion
katie talked about. anyway, we give into
you as you give unto others and somewhere in the
bush is the bush perhaps = the changing frames of
time that once climbed.

**the kingdom of the father is spread upon the earth
&man does not see it**

the lizard's blooded river (tracks) pouring into

a field of movement at the edge

if this is all that's learned

then take it

20

going down the road

he could be blind
points between the last two pick-up trucks
toward a grave, the ohaden cemetery
one of bojangles' names on the cornerstone
a rattler underneath
without being uncovered
the only law of death
he hears
this one
who lives on the living
gabble of geese
human mouths
&blind bodies
ghostwoman with ashes on her breath
the other stories around us
finney blowing sax in memphis
being read below
the white hills/clear rain   stripped
again
(as in ghost love
            what thomas was talking about?)

who is from the same

On Charlie's father's porch—near the arched banks of
Snake River, the four of us hung out drinking gin, rolling dice,
aiming buckshot& .22s. Bojangles always pretending to be
crazy, wearing Katie's dresses, occasionally washing her feet.
Blind shores. Throwing knives& telling lies when our fathers
were pure drunk, gone on inside the gone rivers.

Dismiss the living before you speak about the dead? Ok.
Those outside the word? Such repose in their interruptions. Bo
gave it a good run. Could kick it out in any automobile. Became a passer-by one day. Figs from thistles, grapes from the
thorns. . . Shook us all up the way he slumped over laughing,
then bleeding on the steering wheel, kissing Charlie's secret
hand. Bad-ass mother fucker. Still scatting blind man blues.

. . .

Sometimes they still find him out here on Saturday
nights. After sitting at the lake all night my fathers could come
home with nothing. When we return from the Club they say
he's sleeping by the bones of cow. Bo Riley. Nicknamed him
Bojangles back then, not that he could really dance. But one
of us. Those invited to dinner excused themselves? So go out
to the roads, bring those who you find they'll say. A question
of blood really, the trickster way he used his legs, bragging as
he shuffled two-step in front of the negro barber shop, slicking
back his head. Damn near vain about it, but cool too—cool all
right.

His image holds us as each gauged description eclipses the world. He'll be hooting by the water, dismissed—skinny dipping as Katie skulks Bone Ridge in her old dresses. Coughing the same blood of the fields. The finer haunts near the Spanish church not far from this abandoned railroad station. Going on in the rain. Shucking love. But who can tell you anything about his mouth? That's the real question. The first move was outside the thin frame of the face as if the queen were no more than a photograph.

after the movies

Year ago they gunned him down. This cousin's cousin. Charlie's step-brother too, we don't care if he was black. Or queer. Take a stretch of voices in his hands& hold them for days talking. The praise of some other? The issuing of acts they'll say. It's only a movement& a rest after all. Because when you come from it you go there again. Gunned him down when we stole the Cadillac, killed Scooter J. the boy. Cherry red, custom engine& pure you know, real tempting like the three barrels of sheer delightful moonshine the pick-up mirrored in the trunk. All of that desire. Blues shifting into the soiled bodies. You bring a white evening into the hills, much later the road, this fatigue distorting the mouth& later the eyes. But let me tell you one thing. He was good at cards.

spiders on the delta

Peculiar silent birds. Blue& white. Paradise cawking. Or those freighters we hopped after getting high on the town, fighting Scooter J. and Billy's boys to pass the time. The bastards still rock& roll on the tracks in the rain. Scooter's voice disappearing over the cliff one evening after Charlie pushed him. Seduction not required but suggested when we first yielded to its language. Subtle tones of response. Ghosted boys. Distance carrying in this mystery as much a part of the story as any pathos that surrounds the absence. Restless hood-lums. Rednecks waiting to go somewhere. Finney gearing up his horn. Small change in his pocket. But the one hitting the road carried the real money.

—*go ahead& call me a nigger faggot one more time Scooter, Charlie snaps, pulling back the whip, then flipping black-jack on the hood of Bojangles' pick-up truck since what the left hand does, he wouldn't let the right hand know. . .*

Smoking dope in the yards. Cheap wine& coming home drunk. Changing skins as if into a solitary shape. Bo& then Katie scatting& drinking from the polluted river. Finney shitting his pants from so much crank. Clear whistles that shot out on Saturday nights bringing crackers in from Memphis. Take heed of the passage. Ok. Talking Ohio. A place in the things around them yet the foregrounding isn't enough. Lies. Listening to the d.j. around dawn. Pick out all the pieces they'll say. We lean toward the ambiguity of another's body as if into a promised land we hear but don't believe in. Bo still keeping schedule on the trains when we walk out here, the white girl drawing a circle in the mud where the animals on the hill continue to speak.

the question of whether ghosts really exist

Charlie laid the switchblade by the cliff that night. Then the rain& a needle. A bastard rush up the blood& resolved to take on the other man's body, even its death it seemed, as if Katie could undo him in those high heeled shoes& red lipstick. We ain't going in there Finney says stepping away from Scooter's corpse. Snakes are in that cave& it's bad ju ju man. You're going too far, Charlie. I got a wrong hit& we don't need it no more. He sees Scooter's figure flying over the roof tops with this his first mouthful of death. Red-breasted robins loose in the bush. Bo unbuttons his shirt, shoots the breeze, finishes off the bottle saying no one should live like that, not even Scooter J. how he's been bellied. You killed him Charlie laughs back lying and dousing the pants, then the shirt& socks with gasoline as if nothing could go unclean. Take a look at his loafers. Ain't they cool? You boys can dish it out pretty good for ones who can't take it. Play us a real tune, Finney. Make your girl snappy man.

That was the first time he realized he was personally going blind. Looking over the fields at all that emptiness. Fine rebuke. Charlie tossing branches on the fire in front of the cave. Katie hanging back, glancing over his shoulder, whisper-ing *whoever has ears. . .* Finney flips the pocket Bible in his hands, starts to read. Why did he come out into the desert? Driving in a Cadillac for Christ's sake? Praying in tongues these lovers touching both sides of the silence.

Excuse my expectation. Charlie regards the eye's initiation with distrust, draws himself into the body, its smell& finality. Who's talking deserts, Finney? Smacks the boy on the back of the head while he laughs at his own loneliness. Who do you think's gonna die now? Your girl? It's the ghost we gonna burn. The thing between the dead& living that you got to be careful about. Burning's your only proof. You want Bo to go to the can? He's the one who knifed Scooter. Picks up a rat& holds it by the tail, waving it in front of them. What do you say to that y'all? You want to be a rat? Give me that Bible. You know where the ghost is. Just where you've been persecuted man.

Scooter's body covered with dry leaves, ants, the face going up in a stench as Bo hisses, staggering on his hands& knees in the bush& rising up against the fire. Fuck no, Charlie! I want a drink& something good this time. Charlie up& belts him too—you saw the bastard last night, a god damn rat spirit, Bo!

Spirit my ass (Bo standing tall for once) if he had a ghost I doubt it could even get drunk—some ghosts are blind in the dark. Then heading out on the water so rare, ready to walk it. Meet the rest of Scooter's boys who were coming to collect their dead. Howls out his own name so it would go on in this place.

Just a dried up little dead boy, that's all. Come on with me, Katie.

hicks& goblins

It was one evening a couple weeks later when he jived across the back porch dressed in drag burning kerosene lighting matches as he crossed the tracks in the other story then blazing the river Jesus walking it himself alongside him fires raging across the blue waters almost as if he trucked the whole distance home& needed a drink. Some 53 miles& two mountains no joking matter, right Bo? The truth is they done buried him six days before after he lost enough blood enough times that no one said they'd even recognized him during those final nights. Going on in the rain& the Cadillac& the moonshine& all that desire. Billy's blind boys did him good but there he was. Bo Riley. Still singing against the horn of the steering wheel going on in the other ear a raging black scarecrow saying this solitary one in the bridal chamber. We can't tell you or mention that Katie could if she wanted because she was at their wedding but look at his body man. Finney marking the grave playing homeward down Bojangles fingering Charlie the fat-ass grin heckling as if him being gone all that time was just his way of getting back proving death to fool everybody since knowing the whole world he found a corpse. Always got the last laugh. Strolled into his former kitchen changing skins at a fancy immediately obliging himself to a bowl of fat-back& pinto beans saying they didn't let those enter who wished the fuckin' pharisees. That strong eye for whiskey a little shy around the lips but eventually he picked up the bottle. All of the characters living within him still no one said a word. Images that came into existence before you. Charlie dropped 3 kings& an ace high. Finney offering cousin a roll with the dice& a quick mouth& damned if the next thing he wasn't singing. To himself.

other rivers

Katie& Finney trailed him out the screen door, along the river—down to this station within time. Where no moth comes. Moseyed about the banks a while, across the marks of his& Scooter's graves watching the snakes, awaiting his next move. 'Death,' you say? Hidden in the 'source'? Whose source? A big roller, we figured he might want to do a gig, pick up one of the moccasins, maybe shuffle a deck, cool-hand& all. . . But he just hummed the way the darkness does. Why did you come out into this desert anyway, Bo? Mysteries worthy of mysteries?

They kneeled close to the mud because that's where it's comfortable. Listening. Summing up the territory between us. From morning to evening& from evening until morning. Catching his voices, then his arms& legs damn near flapping between the eucalyptus& pine& the ghosted river.

the big beat

A mockingbird darted out of the wood again last night as if we were still there in the beginning. Ducks& geese almost in conversation (the one we were always missing in the past). Black water eddies along the shore the real cradle daddy Thomas sung them Charlie says appearing sudden& almost completely blind in this light, confused because the story always continues. What the hell you doing here anyway, Bo? I don't need you he says, groping in the dark. Dead fuck! As if all of his own ghosted bodies went flying with that eye. He

spit. Pissed all right. Couldn't see straight. Drunk maybe, but
he pulled his blade, plucked the red bird right out of the limb.
Should have seen it fall. Fast with his arm, Charlie could
always spin a pearl-handle, stick it back-side in a branch before
the blink of any eye. Jesus we loved that.

Depends on a mouth he begins—as if he had discovered
something after all that time.

Not that he was ever one with words, still he might
have said something more—*brother*, for instance—or even,
how 'bout a game of cards for Christ's sake given all these years.
Deep down always ashamed their bloods had mixed, that he
had shared this brother's love.

Cousin made a long hyena into the woods, hawking his
way into the unlit hills, snapping his thumbs as he disappeared
once more beyond the ridge. Started singing, not normal
though. Charlie turned, nodded. Give them what's in your
hands—blind to his own empty hands& watching Katie walk
off behind Bo, pretending to be one of those washing the
outside of the cup. Hills be moved, make what you will of this
mouth.

Say what, Bo?

husbandmen

They still study him nights like this—cold out, rain threatening snow. A kind of delta blues he released to the fields when we practiced horns together& danced. Snow takes its place along the trains. Gray alpine, two windmills in the distance. These scattered miles. Cousin's voice echoing the line of empty boxcars, the carcass pavement off Route 99 where he can lie down when he damn well pleases. This place we call home. Katie stores all of his magazines& shoes over there.

Reminds you of Charlie too sometimes, the four of us fucking off together running up& down these lines—fishing nothing, blue blind& wild on cheap champagne, singing the night changed true.

when the new world comes

somewhere in the obliterated fields

the dead come about

—what do you expect of them?
the towns remain the same though

—secrets in telling?

whoever has known the world has found a corpse
say—

a constancy of two figures walking
along the rivers

finney& katie working the crowded oblique

into these rank tents by the shoreline

vanquished on the day of the harvest
the weeds appear

—tell us then?

swaggering through the cities

how we speak of them as rivers?

of the words
yet unabstracted

III: *eating the voices*

image

—we guard it until it (the world) is
afire

boats on the water by the palace
where the hills crest unevenly

the bare alpine& clear bay
hustling down the urgency of roads this morning

—tell me if you can see the fields
as yourself

oranges, tangerines, insects, walnuts, worms
has all vanished since?

—then wait for the vegetables to die

as in the way we talk about
the switchblade exchange& all that

a way in& out of the suspense

oh blind dog of love& then
alone again

—if they say to you it is in the sea
then the fish will precede you finney

hovering by the staircase
the palace gates open to viewing

—but the kingdom is within&
it is without you

the mingled shadows we consider human
&not ghostlike

along her thighs

katie is the story& past anatomy

our contained desire/
the uncooked flesh

                a single one
                this darker language

                pieces of menstrual blood
                spotted along the banks

make it alive she says

                entering the
                kingdom of the ear

                trouserflies, detective potboilers
                telling your plots

—clues?

walking along the populations
that scatter before us

                watch for the world

goats on the hillside

Something drifted over her head because they weren't listening anymore. Whoever has ears Finney whispers. Katie's old man waiting there. Katie leaning to the left, all done up, her naked back to her daddy& lips quivering, moist—calling the blind ghost perhaps. One of the chosen ones. A small fire in the grove. The blind boys watching. Testing the face of the sky, not knowing its movement. Such a fine wine Finney thinks. A boy now. The worn country fence almost hovering between them. Wretched bodies. Covered with raspberry vines. Empty cans of PBR& busted-up rain bottles of screw you over buddy—my name's Mr. Jim Beam. Finney stares at the railroad tracks separating the land, that long stretch of nowhere breaking light into the hills. Hills be gone he says, not knowing this beginning. A shine of the gun barrel reflecting off the old man's eyes—racoon shadows& the rest of it just waiting for the move. His move. Not by expectation. Did I get that right, Finney? You who go before us.

Katie's daddy taking time, scampering across the porch, slow talk& whistle-like whiskey all over the mouth's gestures, then hollering her name. Over here! Kneel down before us. Make what you will of it Finney would say one day. Our mouths. A communion in the tongue. Striking one, a Lucky straight, a .22 in hand—good& mean. The old man hollering all day long. Baptist man. Yep.

When he finds he'll be troubled. Where now then? A groundhog popped its head to show them it was spring already. A messenger from the morning. And suddenly they went blank together, just like that. Two idiots shooting blood on a target range, spitting hate& weeping Jesus. Holding the other Thomas in their hands. Throw not your pearl before swine Finney smirks. Silver fish set forth on the chopping block for the blind boys. Whoever has ears.

Taking no thought of the morning. Their eyes close nearly touching as an early evening sun appears. The slight haze. Horn of a bull, hoof of a horse sheeting a low horizon. They stood in the distance of her daddy's talk. Small talk. Like so many times autumn rain had changed to snow& here it was seeding time again. Finney's old man had drowned himself that summer. Old Hep. Hep man Thomas. Crocodile daddy all gone. Just the words' worlds remaining. Me talking nonsense, or maybe saying nothing at all as I watched from the ravine. What'd you say to that, son? Who you gonna believe?

Katie reached across once. Hearing this story& the others approaching. Something in the blood. Do you know what you're talking about? Love? She says it again, taking no notice of him. Her own hand real quiet, full, yet slow in the silence. Outline of something lost already showing in the bone, the tiny black fingers, the voice's blue hesitation. Hell. Can't say it twice, sister. Never could. Just love. Finney trembles, the way you do before pulling the trigger, then chasing after the fall. Original smile on her face as he raises the gun barrel. Rubbing the pistol like the fur of an unborn— her hair on his blood. Sexy. Almost. Not the taste of death. Not in these mouths.

I mean the opposite of fate, Finney. The one who chose this eye. All of them before you. Each moment. Her daddy shot high to remind her. Sot's shot gun blast—chase him away, hey boy. Reminds Finney about the gospel of his daddy. *Blasphemy boy—telling you son. Straight to hell Hep goes just like you behind him. Him pretending to be one of Jesus' chosen fishers.*

Dead Sea floating on his back Finney yells back.

He laughs, ready then. And all a sudden he wanted to catch the things Katie muttered before/so we went off together in the planted fields thinking maybe there'd be a sign like Hep's final words—blessed the lion which the man eats& the lion will become man& cursed the man who the lion eats& the lion will become man. Daddy always said it like that Finney laughs again. After all, he figured they were still out there somewhere, didn't you Finney—the words, their sounds like bunched up ramblers just heading out on the trains, or flapping in some other woman's yard like all the clean shirts hanging on that clothes line? A little Blues cheer you up, boy? Listen to the hoboes. Finney holds Katie sure, taking his own aim, shooting once for that part of her old man he hated most, remembering the mattress& the wine& the black shoes. Later adding three more pieces of metal to the head. You could have knelt down dammit! No more turn aside& brood.

Stand at the beginning. Their nights on the river is what I miss most—before he came into being, swimming the dark. Thin arms wrapped up like that. Where the beginning is there's the end? Naked by the shore, the cool grass, jasmine, a smell of turpentine& the way she squeezed him hard. I guess she liked fishing, making love Christian style. That was fine. But Finney couldn't meet her by that plot of tobacco forever, fearing his sex, the blind boys, that steel of boot-leg 'round

40

back. Her bad-ass brothers& staggering through those screen
doors spitting to kick his ass. (Doing more than that if it
wasn't for you, Charlie). Themselves in a field now. They take
off their clothes to release it. He was so scared looking at the
image that the blood itself was easy. Murderer of scarecrows.
Finney ran as fast as he could, trying to wave down the love
moving with the freights all the way out here—this dry desert
heat.

What's the name of this town?

What is the opposite
of your riddle with eyes
See I am all the Woman
Eurydice who got bitten
by the snake but was
the snake herself, I am
all those dream transformations
in the pool at midnight that one of our
friends tending guard letting us
swim over each other let us if

all vanished since

      Hey Charlie. What about that butcher's blade? Shit.
You can't knife your own dreams. Ever since we were kids,
you've been hating the world. Drunk tonight, wanting to
cross that swinging bridge& kill somebody. Jumping rattler
pits all day just to prove you're lucky. Spitting at the moon.
Diving Snake River, sharp& naked as the stars. I see you all
right. Still got that one blind eye, don't you, Charlie? Hardly
recognize your own name. Always crazy, so put away the
blade.

      Listen, those are our brothers fishing the eddies,
      breathing the night cotton, Bo& Finney whis-
      tling glory down the bank. The other you's.
      They ain't gonna hurt nobody. Each one's got
      water running in his voice. Hear 'em call out—
      Jesus, whatcha doing over there. Hey Jesus,
      here's the spot! Of course that's your name. As
      memory gauged it. Sure it is. And we're bound
      to be fishers. But breaking the biggest silence,
      they swagger in the mud, humming mosquito
      music, wading the moss edge with six packs&
      flashlights. Shadows among shadows. Blind
      boys. Just kin come out on a Saturday night,
      Charlie—that's all.

      So pull that harmonica. And mean tunes. Rats
under the bridge. Hoot all hell if you want, you cock-eyed
bastard. They'll listen& leave us alone. No reason to worry.

This is the true part. Nothing but cool-ass jazz, whiskey dark. God becomes woman becomes fish becomes bird becomes flying. . . Easy blowing rifts. Toss me that horn. They're pitching line now. See 'em skimming the whiteness, crossing the river, touching hands. Come on. You ready? We'll dance.

early rain

Later that evening a small fire as you leaned against the river bank, tilting the empty canteens, talking about how you wanted to touch me the way we both touched Katie—easy& close, rubbing your hands, staring at my shoulders, curling your legs toward the rocks, looking for cigarettes to hide this fear. The cliffs rising behind you. The Mississippi's current pulled in the miles from Tennessee through Missouri—up past the Ozarks where we splashed in its coldness. Struggling once, you slung a piece of river across shore after I shoved your head below the blueness& held it longer than either of us expected. Breaking free you finished the day's wine, hollered at the boxcars rolling again—this time without us. We couldn't catch on, but spoke to the weeds, thinking about Katie& that abandoned farmhouse we awoke to early the next morning, thirsty& broke off a highway near St. Louis, watching the cars go by. Drunk on the side of the road before dawn, you just wanted to sleep.

Against the remaining sun we forgave the morning, the old gospels, Hep Thomas& then the coal tracks that curved into a blackening mountain. . . Like the funny world we were finally leaving, the rock ridges drew the quiet in. No stars but your harmonica blessed the distance, our last Drum, Katie's shared bodies, the closing August day—as if hearing the same notes over& over persuaded me. Still shivering, half-naked by the flames I lifted my arm& saluted the last train, that Northern& Western line, the highway alongside it. Then the red caboose sudden& like fables in childhood. The sky behind it joining the bits of darkness.

garden of the maps

stealing between their lives
he sees his own reflection
days about the place
a child's broken mouth
the mirror
two women nearby
what is hidden revealed
he reaches for the snaked God
the age of their faces
fine
inner hands up
&under
the coral skirts
full of small fish
struggling
finney notices the cold lines
appearing&
his own face blooms
says what goes into your mouth will not defile you
shunning afterwards
the woman he'll eventually
become

imagined waters

traveling the real is no easier
the popular folklores abandoned

within them

fishing out the eye
a sustained love (parting) this grave

purging the emotional no longer fits you finneys

the torched lanterns hanging years ago
our childhood blessed curse

a noose around bo's throat
at snake river

or the other skins
burned snakes exploding in the fire of this bush

diverse roads
like common roads on the map to more roads

bring the clan removed from history out of its cave

thomas says

tragedy a shattering of the forms
&their attachment to them

46

sober at last
katie turns to the bluest air

we touch blackened skin

kiss the only mouth

IV: *ripe air*

image

after the burning
we don't have to stop

singing into
a separate lung

your own hands humbled such as these

silences known to all

embarrassed you take off your clothes
without being ashamed

the soul pretends to be the body

we don't care if you ever figure it out

these real ones in the bush finney

singing itself a blooded code

two worlds that could be one
vanishing points in the flames

three sources

the boss of the horse is a friend of mine?
i'll never concede that. security he says.
not mine though. blackness. blackness in the
vanishing points. bo understood that. tonight
i'm pushing everything away. i did it all day
but tonight vicious about it. jaundiced even.
working here won't cut no finney gonna
take that line. when it is noble in the blood the
boss says. like we can't sing the blues.
change the laws. katie's dress hanging low as
she passes the stable. got your letter
charlie. but there will be no purging. no
saxophones. why don't you ask her out he says?
my wife. your sister. for the both of us in that way.
or at least before. love ain't the word for it now.
she don't need a career either i told him.
invisible here. the field vanishing too.
like the temples we walked away. should
see her play dust angels& dance charlie.
not like a has been. no. he isn't my friend. or the
others. just blinded is all. i saw her roll away
from him. thought he might be feeling guilty.
pushed on the screen door like he was entering
a church. his pants still undone. exaggerating?
i'll leave it at that. you know the stories. they have
their own charlie.

wichita state psych ward

Sometimes I get so desperate for love I run down the street with my cock in my hand. Look out over the buses to see if she's there. Stare down all the shiny black cars like a coal miner just up for the light. Crazy when the longing comes, quiet, late in the evening—alone between the sheets. No automobiles. I spot the moon's blood& think of home, the old temple, the Jesus freaks running speed in the woods. The city sounds hold tight blue blood sleep, terrifying like the empty tin cup on my pillow. Where are you Charlie. Come back you can't die. *Shit on you preacher. You don't know love.* The way baby squeezed me hard, waist first, then thighs, down the deformed marks on my neck where she burned me drifting that deep reach into her god domain. I burn everything& it ain't what counts. Reach for the lamp but it's no use. No one's there. Cry her name over& over again. Jacking-off 'til nothing's left of the skin. Smoking heroin like the rich boy art-fucks at Fat's Bar, sipping bad-ass Jim Beam. Bang it against the wall& *fuck you too doctor.* Mornings I eat eggs& try to forget, writing bastard ballads about the dead, seeing her face all jazzed up, drinking coca-cola, smoke in hand, leaning off the edge of the bed, nothing but the smell of her thin muscles smothering my face, her fish-white back better than no drug, no fuckin' rock& roll jazz blues club numbers shit game mister. I burn everything& it ain't what counts. Burn your god damn house down if you touch her. Her nakedness, a smell of panties lingers in my clothes. I walk to work everyday trying to wear it out, shake it down, horny—but not as loud as the rooster the boys keep in the junkyard out back. I could cut his balls off every time he starts fucking—just out of envy. Just like Katie did when I refused her. Just like you Charlie.

solitary ones

At just the right intersection there is no face, only his body, drifting forward. Floating almost, somewhat contorted—toward the table where Charlie's last letter sits by the ashtray, causing him to think of a chopped off ear in the shadows of the early morning. A chopped off ear? His own perhaps, at least that's the way it strikes Finney as he kneels on the floor, trying to remember how he got here. Who chose this face for me he asks. As if for the last time? The only thing he can remember now is Scooter Johnson's boys throwing him against the wall, slicing away his ear, taking the little money left and tossing his things out the backdoor, threatening to cut off his faggot balls next time. Scooter's boys carried away his horn& guitar. Because there are secret words& whoever finds their explanation will not taste death.

Finney rises to the table eyes darkened, elbows trembling, peering over the envelope& broken bottles, trying to find his way back from where the beginning is. Come on Finney you can do it. This old terrain. Tucked deep in his bruised skin. Finney sees himself in the other worlds for a moment, blowing sax, dreaming this. He wants to pick up Charlie's letter, shake out the words like the missing ear. Caress the lobes, shuck the words& bones out the kitchen window where all of his clothes& books lie in piles by the garbage. The dead mouths. Where ears stand waiting. But he can't understand his life, where the stories are leading him.

Charlie's letter begins—brother, lover, mistress? When you take off your shame no one puts it under a bush.

Taking no thought from morning until evening& from evening until morning for what he puts on, Finney says, you retarded mother fucker. Yet hearing the voice, the body remembers itself. I don't want you here, get out of my life, Charlie. Go on& fuck yourself on bad flesh& junk—daily news from the massage parlor sluts who'll never love you. Finney thinks of the man turned woman as he circles the kitchen, the one he left lying in a northern river to drown like his own old man. Thinks of the lover he grew up with& believed in, the one who tried to kill him one night because Finney couldn't accept the confusion of merged bodies.

He looks through the broken glass of the kitchen window, touches the cuts left on his face earlier by Scooter's boys, fondles the old burns sister Katie gave to his throat. Finney knows Charlie's dead, this one he never wanted except inside him like his own blood or the beginnings& he thinks of the nights he slept on Charlie's shoulder afraid of everything that moved, afraid of his own sleep& how Charlie could calm him then, saying my mouth will not be capable.

Finney prays nothing to the old brother, the moon he troubled under, the plot he's been born into—unaware of his own face, the throat, the burns, his only physical memory of voice. He walks past the table to the refrigerator, opens the morning prescription. Whoever has ears to hear let him hear. *Say what, Charlie?* He catches himself. Looks at the maps of the Dead Sea plastered to the cabinet walls, his own mountain. Calmly sucks down the handful of reds& bennies he's awakened to every day for the past month. Empties the glass of milk, takes an extra handful today, stares at the eyes from the cruxificion that stare back from the living room wall. A first smoke and the Albuquerque Tribune on this day he decides to die. The day he becomes Thomas. Starts the naming that leads into.

Finney blowing shit-faced in a Memphis bar the first night we found him. Just one of the readings. This son of a half-black preacher& a working man. A father who killed himself in the early evening summer heat on July 19, 1955, just in time for the boys& Katie to see the old Pentecostal daddy rolling into the river, huge-bodied, guitar like a vest clung to his chest, singing the kingdom of the father, he draws the sword in his house, sticks it in the wall to know if his hand will carry through, then slays the powerful fuck... Later the boys would make up lies about what they saw, inventing something new every time, never really sure if what they saw was Finney's daddy or not, Thomas the Doubting Disciple or a devil or an incarnation of their past. Perhaps just another ghost, already drowned in the body because it was so big, over 7 feet tall, unable to contain itself. Finney picks up the old man's notebooks he's saved all these years, images him once more. The desire that flowed into this face, the face he almost feels now, into the embraces that surprised even Katie.

He slides the envelope off the table, reads the return address, wonders about Charlie's funeral& whether attending the services could ever be the last horn. Wonders if Katie will be there. This is how it ends or begins, the story& its telling— the imagined as well as the real, where the two intersect& what we remember of it all anyway. That part of me that was him, the part of him that was us, filling in the rest because the telling is what's left = the anatomy of these blind tongues almosting it& drinking from a scorched mouth.

what hep man thomas told finney& bo the night he drowned in snake river

what's wrong with the world is people ain't got enough
money& the ones that do don't know how to spend it right&
if somebody starts singing good anyway cityfolks try to buy it&
if the music brings a hard price we lose another singer like
those little children who have installed themselves in a field
which is not theirs& if you think there are enough good
singers it's like a mustard-seed smaller than all seeds so just
take a good look around or come stumbling down this river say
any friday night where there used to be plenty of us gathering
and hardly no radios or take my buddies for example sitting in
a barn that's only got more whiskey than lies yet when you
make the two one and when you make the inner as the outer
so that the male will not be male and the female not female or
when you make eyes in the place of an eye& a hand in the
place of a hand& a foot in the place of a foot then you shall
enter but they're still talking about who they could have been
playing with those nashville records so you can just walk
yourself down to town where everybody's dressed up
pretending to be somebody else's clothes while the outer& the
inner& the above is below us and when you make the male
and the female into a single—well you see there's just strangers
like you& me picking by ourselves trying to figure this river
out

before bo's murder on july 4th

what i'm good at
i've never wanted

lost in the water
—scallop of st. james

see that sun?

what comes out of your mouth
that's what defiles you

while traipsing on a distant road
he breathed his spirit into

another mouth

blinded to the past
(give it to me now)

we roll into the future
forgetting our names

highway 29

he retires humming to his sisters

together they write hymns& occasionally dance

the worms ate them long ago

but their slick tunes

the stones will burn you up man

V: backwaters

image

burnt out& over-drugged
they sleep

the death of the tin-can men

so that their eyes won't be broken

—it's impossible to say finney
the crossing at the rivers frozen

the snowed brick lanes

letting stories back in
from the hillsides

—you got the keys to the truck bo?

(some evening wine)

—yeh, a fine automobile he says

grasshoppers around the surrounding path

distance entering the absent mouths

suddenly
passers-by

the natural urge of
a monday morning good-morning

on earth as it is in heaven

evening finding itself

i don't like to meet
for dinners anymore
—where now?

they've become too formal& dull

neck of the horse, back of the snake
perhaps under the bridge charlie
—where the old man drowned?

signs on a white field
black birds

an image in place of the image

good enough then
let the rats have us

spooky

these prayers

      the open tracks converging

in another ear

speckled snakes blinded along the roadside

reigning over all

singing st. james

look at the world
it occurs

—whoever drinks from this mouth

not its happening
but where to fit in or
do anything about it

—remember how thomas lied?

not a chance operation
the finishing of any act
is like that finney

no one else around
the shifting eyes

tooting in the back room
hitting the high keys

taking a drink& kicking back

all these things moving about

the imagined growing into
its own rhythm

66

be you a bean or a stalk
hallelujah then

those yet
uptown drums
still unplowed

undrum them

he chose the large fish without regret

Trying to understand it like this, Finney. Reserved yet about to yield. More often than not a memory& incarnation no better than the lives creating them. A mustard seed. Three blind mice. How often this doesn't matter anymore. Always forgiven but we piss on forgiveness& this genuinely bothers me. Horsepiss. Sour wine. A lot of evenings nothing but banjo tunes. Fine. A blackened cart laid along her thighs. Clogging over this plowed soil& occasional hymns. These kin eating the dried loaves of bread, their secret bodies. I know for a fact God's holding nothing against us. Told me so. Like when the hoeing's done& you can fall in the hard rows of tomatoes, potatoes& peas. Reclaiming the love not past but constantly born in our mouths. Sometimes it don't bother to hurt. We tell ourselves this over& over—you shall enter. Lost in the waters. God is love& loves all things the other Thomas, your Aquinas, said. Remember Finney. The fishtrap on New Year's Eve. You're no baby no more but you know my lives. Nights I held my own, listening as if a part of the sounds. Shout a few flying rifts as they pass. The way the river does becoming a single one. Or hearing it from the porch& drinking black wine by the tracks you once rode to Ohio. All those years. Troubled ain't the word for it. Misguided& admitted my wrong. Considering myself a mouth, a preacher, a giver of words. Still him, crocodile king& true Thomas all along. Mostly trying to expose these fears so I couldn't hide them from myself. Telling your stories in the garden of the rot. A pure fool either way. Who chose these eyes for us you ask? Scrambling for love on the tracks, along back alleys, pool halls, hardly existing night clubs. Bedrooms of friends& their wives& let me tell you the taste of shame. It was leaving that saved this mouth. No more turn aside& brood? Hearing you cry on a boxcar. I still dream of all that walking home drunk& the others can tell you I was good at it.

Crickets make better song still we live a ways from where they teach you to do things pretty. My 12th rib gone. Among the fanshoal of fishes. The sacrifice. One of the boys always boasting about last year's rain among the living. Miss it? Or the someone. On the spoons. No longer choking on the angeled songs. A man drowned. Music hooted as if from the face of an owl. Clicking tongues on a Jew's harp. Slapping against the wheelbarrow to catch the ringing of horns. Evening will find itself with or without you, Finney. Horning it. A hint of mandolin gets the old man cupping his hands around a churchbell like a wine sucker juicing blues God only knows how. Ghostwoman in the cupboard. You know me, Finney? Release it to our fields then. Bet a dime no fool is whistling before we get a chance. The one who came before you. Why? How the stars that surround our field remind me of love if I'm in a good mood. Why not? Why do you ask?

All vanished since? Look around. I don't know what to tell you. These hands, their mouth, whose movements. Taste death. Fat legged corn brush one another chattering like palms over a washboard. A light breeze. Watch for the world. Dance better when the owners come, boy. Even a scarecrow's legs kick to a bunch of strong laughs. Empty you in& out of the world, Finney. Fires grow across the roads. Pour out of their mouths. At ease with a life in a straight cool air cooing summer night. Can't tell you origins. Only that it won't come by expectation. I saw a face only once but in more ways than one. Drum. I had no idea I was going to be your daddy. Darkness in darkness remember hands& their source. You know how hard it is for you Finneys to talk about love. You were just beside us one morning. Then all of these musicians came stepping out of their barns = time came over here, clean-shaven, ready—maybe whiskeyed up, staggering as if still in dream& there was nothing to it. Nothing to it.

six days gone

sometimes he thinks he could hunker down in this basement
for weeks, maybe get drunk& sleep until friday. but things
keep doing what they want. she& finney pace the edge of the
clock—arms akimbo& there's this shrilled music of love
mystifying no one. it's nothing spectacular. love not
yet the pain of love. not a love in capital letters. but the kind
that leaves little worms on the floor. voodoo kisses. quick swaps.
dancing fools. where the light originated& revealed itself in their
image. two people trying to hug from opposite corners of the room.
what they find between themselves was never lost to begin with.
but try explaining something like that. a vine has been planted.
all the same it's 10 a.m. &nobody's called. katie says lay down, he
wakes up, then they hum it like in the talk shows, the good ones
where everybody's got a lot to say& not enough time.
put new wine in old wineskins? finney thinks what
the hell& dials up for another gig. burns him up the way they
spit in the phone. patience in the eye. he might be selling
bananas by evening. or waxing horns. can do damn near
anything. howl a tooting sax even after it all. charlie will
tell you that much. watch him tap dance on the linoleum
floor. let him show you what they can do.

lament

sand sifting sideways without the movement of feet

when the morning begins we find

our first thirst

sliver fish you set forth on the chopping block

an older thomas out there

the way he preached to the river

a rowboat leaning against the dock

the split oars

an absolute calm

blue water, black sky

ritual of the eaten

notes toward their reappearance

simply yourself
no more pouting sister

born within
choose the always&

create death
the water's shoreline& evening
fishing

suffering enraptured in process

a first strip in the clean-out
die not a moment before it

faith in the way we care for the world

a dwelling content
i& the small leaves at the edge of your tongue&

joyous participation

the moon slight tonight
embodying the river's shallowed&

flowed deception

72

(re) entering   like this
on the lizard's impulse

only as good as the grasslands

then the bodies

&this active difficulty

VI: *kingdom of the elect*

image

after he went out of being

possibility of other tongues

not over but in this ruptured hour

gestures in the absence of a mouth

locating smaller bones

going into your navel

sharing the highway sounds

mustard seeds in her field

the difference between those
coming&
those going
requires a look at the hands
alive in the world
the dog barks when one comes or goes
if a response is necessary
go to the bone
smell our blood
what is appearance
&absence combined
finds itself here
among the corpses

. . .

an open mouth
knows what is enough
look inside
the blind speaking
a possibility of
speaking   the body's fields
stripped
&calling in this ridge of hills

alone   look again
sacrifice of the stoned pavillion
listen for
the eye's flicker& these sheep
gathering outside the rain
expansive steppes   shallowness of the stream
                &then
sun& stars&
romance you want to touch
what strikes within   the interior
of the nose's hair/   breath& impulse
when anyone comes or goes

. . .

what we see is not at this garden's edge
black ants crawling
about the sleeve
into your socks
somewhere we possess
a nowhere
whose God& love present
can't say it
a troubled affair&
without language as the mirage enters
to live in the deer as she runs toward
the hunter's call
our drunkenness&
crossing between the crushed stones
dusted heaps of gone grasslands
though death
begins
past their fields

. . .

these are the unspoken details
born out of so many days
walking
the vanishing skies& what follows
as the rains close in
thomas, why have you come so far
to hear so little
only the drowned
fish remain
in the waters do we
find such articulate difference
nothing comparable to emotion
because we know that outside it
we have no being

. . .

the
world   bends
the curtains
&converses the mirror
along the tracks
maybe her corpse
sustaining because
in this way
there is no shit beyond us
the test we set for them
they have passed
what country have they come from
find a moment
&smoke in it
if this is
all we have
celebrate the hour

of saying who you are like

the way finney rolled over& awoke in a different body.
thinking about time& how it loses itself in the blind mouths.
the changes& shifts of dream that go unnoticed in gesture.
pictures of you by the river we've seen over& over. this story,
the one already known& outside memory. we find ourselves in
it long enough to pick out the broken glass, glance to the left,
watch the phrase the worlds have long imagined. all gone
where? vertical air, parching heat, decay. he who walked the
waves alreadying& empty. yet you finneys gather some things.

finney intermittently swept up in this boat. the cargo carries
rot oranges, tangerines, gnawed walnuts. cliffs obliterated in a
blue heat. black steamers in the northern lights& these naked
boys swimming on the shore. absence in the plot causes them
to think of themselves. how the images continue. wilderness
moan by these deserted continents. who we've become
traveling the questionable identities. open eyes, dry stones,
flower of an unseen color. charlie striking a match to a small
kerosene light warming the hands, a single piece of bread. his
hope to survive the river goes on here. ghostwoman. ashes on
her breath. sand& stone& shells. what remains of the open
palms.

the earlier one so much opposed to morning light. his eyes
trailing across the water. dripping of the faucet as you sit on
the stool drying those hands. porcupines& squirrels in the
meadow. as the dead come about the love each drum plays.
looking at you from such deep graves. he'd rather do it like this
if necessary. solitude of cold afternoons. shared tea. the bodies
joining further in the unclosed fields. under the hills a forward
whiteness. scored light as music& the windows out into this
cleared darkness. bushweed& roof tops conducted along the
sloped horizon. a lone owl becoming the single one.

always this falling off to sleep in the middle. not a regret& not
a dreaming. the old thomas who sat beside us on the bed.
fish& seaweed smell mapping the sand. unrealized source. all
of the othering. each action arises by itself. 12 apostles having
preached to all the gentiles. worlds without end. their
fascination with knives connecting in loneliness for all that
comes. or pure destruction. form of forms which darkness could
not comprehend as memory unfolded it. of saying who you are
like. taste of death. the slow rite. bo donning his cap, dancing
by the blues guitar. saxophones horning the secret air, hidden
rivers. deep song of violent hands as ants cover us over& over.
warned against the complaining, celebrate the hour. play
it right then. walking finney from late evening to early
dawn& can we ever know this. the path obliterates
each bitter mystery.

tourists playing tennis in tan shorts across the beach. katie
drinking heineken this the first of every morning. black spots
in front of a blue sea. see it now. so distinct they're hardly
visible anymore. an image like vacations when she cuts the
stones. fearing jellyfish, all that can be witnessed in shallow
water. sailboats. even her distance narrowed. because disaster
is easier, predictable. seaweed floating to the beach. she combs
her hair. the body pretends. but this is only one face.
blackwater riverish again& forever in the brewing katie. now
we understand. sit calmly. wait. she looks into the reflection
the others gave her. partakes in every prayer staring back. so
much a fire in the ending. every century. her mouth is capable.
silver fish she set forth on the chopping block. singing.
&merging with the scenery. too quiet for her own liking some
mornings yet without resistance, perhaps. no longer desperate
in the troubles found. worship the time remaining. rain in it.
the slow growth& rain (reign) of rite.

mystery for waters. catfish& perch. cool wind eating the
beginning without end. drives them crazy when we forgive
ourselves. standing by the story. the characters incomplete&
washing hands. the new tunes no different. say finney. thicket
of brush, exposed sunset. maybe it's not the small shark charlie
witnessed in the net while running across the deck. just the
likeness of ourselves shedding near the edge of each false start.
fear left alone for a moment as you wanted to reach out for the
fin, the reefs pulling up again toward savage fields. others did
it. other mouths. human shells. nearing it. this love. dry fog&
the skins becoming fish.

communion of human bodies that precede them now. lining
the shore you were sure of that. small cities disappearing past
the hills. thomas in ghostshoes found drowned. sign of a white
field. whose cultures? burrowing in. whose times? snakeskin.
whose logics? determining each sequence? none now. whoever
finds has no explanation. fanshoals, minnows, seaburns. the
known word. morning moves itself in& without him.
photograph of the worlds. carcass meat& hanging skulls. walk
lightly we say. as if deciding the location for a picnic. for
anything. blue air breath. foreign voices later& always pull
awake dark songs coming up to meet them. strolling in a
cotton shirt. meshed in the narrative that reminds each corpse.
pieces of driftwood. octopus, shrimp, prompt repulse&
scavenger blood. this price. what then? what the world wants
when it finds itself. finney's repose. dismissed in the
suddenness. ants gnawing each eye. so they will not be broken.